I WAS CHASING RAINBOWS BUT SHOULD HAVE BEEN CHASING GOD!

by

Maricia Duhart

duhartbooks@gmail.com

I Was Chasing Rainbows but Should Have Been Chasing God!

Copyright © 2024 by Maricia Duhart

Printed in the United States of America

ISBN: 979-8-218-45660-3

Published by Joseph's Ministry, LLC
(www.josephsministryllc.com)

All rights reserved. No part of this publication may be reproduced, distributed, or transmitted in any form or by any means, including photocopying, recording, or other electronic or mechanical methods, without the prior written permission of the author except in the case of brief quotations embodied in critical reviews and certain other noncommercial uses permitted by copyright law.

Debra's rainbows consists of relationships, friendships, spirituality, spirits, creativity and growth until she had a breakthrough. Debra's breakthrough made her decide she wanted to embrace a persovnal relationship with God, and the best course of action to achieve this was through deliverance. Debra comes to realize through her deliverance comes gifts.God brought Debra's gifts back to the forefront due to her obedience. Debra surrounded herslef with her spiritual family and let go of those influences that encouraged the sin. Debra had one friend who prayed for her and never abandoned her through her roughest patches of life.

Home

INT. BEDROOM

Debra is asleep in her bed covered up with a red comforter. Her dog is asleep in its bed. The camera zooms in on the clock on the nightstand. The time on the clock reads 1:00am.

Debra wakes up and looks at the clock

                    DEBRA
            (Debra stretches and
             yawns)
      Oh my gosh, why am I awake so
      early.

Debra gets out of bed, takes a cigarette and lighter out of her nightstand drawer. Her dog gets up from its bed. There are two phones on the nightstand. She picks up both phones and walks to the kitchen. The dog follows her to the kitchen. Debra opens the refrigerator door and grabs a beer. She walks outside into the backyard and sits in a chair. The dog sits beside her on the ground.

EXT. BACKYARD

Debra sits down, opens beer and lights cigarette. Debra looks through one of the cellular phones. Camera zooms in on the phone text messages.

>   (Maliah: I miss you so
>   much, and the love we
>   made made me realize how
>   much I miss you.)
>
>   (Ex- girlfriend:I loved
>   making love to you. I
>   know you have been in a
>   relationship with Debra
>   for seven years, but I
>   want you back.)
>
>   Maliah: I am going to
>   make that happen)

                    DEBRA
              (starts to cry)

Debra picks up her cellular phone and dials Vera's phone number.

INTCUT PHONE CONVERSATION

                    VERA
          Hello?

                    DEBRA
          Hey Vera, what are you doing?

INT. VERA'S BEDROOM

Vera sits up in her bed. Her son lies next to her with her arms across her leg.

                    VERA
          I just woke up and this boy is all
          over me. The real question is, why
          are you awake?

Vera looks over at the clock on her nightstand.

                    VERA
          It is 1:40 in the morning. What's
          wrong?

DEBRA
Remember when I told you Maliah left her cell phone at the airport. The airport called me, and said they mailed the phone to the house. I saw her messages.

VERA
Don't tell me everything you suspected is true.

DEBRA
Yes

VERA
What the heck! Are you leaving her? I know if I were you, I would have been left her and those dogs. I'm sure her neighbors would have loved to take care of them until she returned home.

DEBRA
She will be home in a few days I will talk to her about the phone messages then.

VERA
What are you going to say?

DEBRA
I don't know yet.

VERA
(makes sound,"woo" and shakes her head)
I still suggest you leave those dogs. You have done so much for her. Girl, she got life messed up.

DEBRA
Granted she did cheat on me. I am not making any excuses for her behavior. But she has also done a lot for me.

VERA
(rolls her eyes)
Okay, it sounds like you are making excuses for her. I am getting ready to go back to bed. You need to try to get some sleep too.

DEBRA
Okay, I will.

Debra and Vera hang up the phone.

INT. BEDROOM

The dog lies in its bed. Debra sits on the edge of the bed. She puts the phones in her nightstand drawer along with her cigarettes and lighter. She lies on the bed and covers herslef up.

Debra wakes up, sits up in bed and looks at her clock. The clock reads 3:00am. Debra gets up and walks outside.

EXT. BACKYARD

Debra leans against a column in the backyard and looks up at the dark sky.

>   DEBRA
> God,I know I am not supposed to
> question you. I just don't
> understand. I have been nothing but
> good to Maliah.

>   DEBRA
>   (eyes widen and Debra
>   looks shocked.)

>   GOD (V.O)
> Move out of the way

>   DEBRA
>   (In a whisper)
> Wow! I have never heard God's
> voice.

INT. BEDROOM

Debra gets into bed and covers herself up in her comforter.

The sun shines through the window. Debra wakes up and gets out of bed. She opens her nightstand drawer and

pulls out Maliah's phone. She puts it in her pocket.

INT. KITCHEN

Debra starts a pot of coffee.

                                                    CUT TO:

INT. FRONT ROOM

Maliah walks through the front door. Debra enters from the kitchen with a coffee mug in her hand.

>   DEBRA
> Good morning Maliah

MALIAH
(puzzled look on her
face)
Good morning. I am hungry. Do you have any breakfast ready?

DEBRA
No, but I do have some questions. Like, where is your cell phone? Maliah sits down on the sofa.

MALIAH
(sighs)
I think I left it at the airport. I didn't want to tell you because I didn't want you to be mad and tell me how irresponsible I am. I've also decided to visit Shariah and her daughter. I want to have a relationship with her.

Debra sips coffee from her coffee cup. Debra takes Maliah's cell phone out of her pocket. She throws it on the sofa next to where Maliah sits.

DEBRA
I suggest for the next person you cheat on, make sure you put a lock on your phone.

MALIAH
Why did you go through my phone?

DEBRA
Why did you cheat on me? If you wanted to be with your ex, why didn't you just say it? You have wasted seven years of my life, time I cannot get back. I looked at you as my forever.

MALIAH
I never looked at you as my forever. I didn't even want you to move in with me seven years ago. I was fresh out of a relationship with my ex. You didn't give me a chance to see if it would work out between me and her. You were in the way.

DEBRA
You encouraged me to move in and helped me move my things. You know what, all I have left to say is that this relationship is over. I'm done!

EXT. BACKYARD

Maliah sits down at the patio table and puts her head down into her hand.

INT. BEDROOM NIGHT

Debra opens the closet door. She takes clothes out of the closet and puts them on her bed. She grabs her suitcase and puts clothes inside.

Debra sits on the edge of her bed. She takes a deep breath, then takes her phone from the nightstand and makes a call.

          DEBRA
Hey Vera, I wanted to call and give you an update. I am moving out tomorrow. I found a place in the City, and the moving company will be here in the morning. I'm scared.

          VERA
It is okay. It's about time you left. Make sure you take time for yourself before getting involved with anyone. Wait, how did you get a place and a moving truck so fast?

          DEBRA
I already made up my mind I was leaving. It was God's voice I heard telling me, I need to move out of the way. What did I do and where did I go wrong?

          VERA
You didn't do anything wrong and none of this is your fault. She made a choice to cheat and not the other way around.

          DEBRA
Thank you. Well, I am getting ready for bed. I love you.

          VERA
Good night. I love you too.

Debra goes to bed.

INT. BEDROOM - DAY

Debra wakes up at 3:00am. Debra sits up in bed, grabs a cigarette out of the nightstand drawer, and walks to the door.

INT. KITCHEN

Debra walks into the kitchen opens the refrigerator and picks up a beer, close the refrigerator door and then walks ooutside.

EXT. BACKYARD

Debra opens her beer and takes a drink. She lights her cigarette and takes a puff. She looks up at the sky. The sky appears to be rainbow colors.

>   DEBRA
> God, I don't know what is
> happening. It seems as though
> everything is happening so fast. I
> also know you are in control of
> everything, but this hurts.

Debra puts out her cigarette and finishes up her beer.Debra goes back into the house.

INT. BEDROOM

Debra sits on the edge of her bed and places her cell phone in the nightstand drawer. She lies down, covers herself up, and goes to sleep.

EXT. DRIVEWAY - DAY

Debra is in the driveway. A moving truck is parked in the driveway. The movers push a dolly from the driveway to the front porch. Debra leads the way back in the house.

INT. BEDROOM

>   DEBRA
>   (Debra has one hand on
>   her hip and points to
>   things around tthe room)
>
> I need you to pack up
> everything in this room
> and drop them off at
> this address.

Debra hands the movers a piece of paper.

>   MOVERS
>   (nod "okay" and start
>   picking up boxes)

Debra grabs her purse and whistles for her dog to come. Debra's phone rings. Debra answers her phone.

>   DEBRA
>   (Into phone)
>   Hello?

                    CHRISTIANA (V.O)
          Hello, how are you doing? I haven't
          heard from you in over two weeks.

                    DEBRA
          A lot has been going on. I am
          moving to the city. As we speak. My
          things are being packed and loaded
          onto a moving truck and I am
          getting ready to head to my car and
          head out. I will call you back in a
          few minutes.

                    CHRISTIANA (V.O)

          Yes, please do.

INT. INSIDE OF THE VEHICLE

Debra gets into her vehicle and her dog follows behind her
and jumps into the back seat.

Debra calls Christiana

                    DEBRA
               (Into phone)
          Hey Christiana

                    CHRISTIANA
          What happened?

                    DEBRA
          She cheated on me

                    CHRISTIANA (V.O.)
          Text me your address. I am on my
          way. Be there in three hours.

                    DEBRA
          Okay. I'll see you soon. I'll text
          you the address as soon as I stop
          somewhere.

Debra hangs up the phone.

EXT. PARKING LOT

Debra gets out of her vehicle. Her vehicle is parked in the
parking lot of a convenience store. Debra walks to the front
of the store.

INT. CONVENIECE STORE

Debra opens the refrigerator and grabs a pack of beer. At
the cash register, she points and a pack of cigarettes
behind the counter. The cashier pulls the pack of cigarettes
down from the wall and places it on the counter. The cashier
rings up the pack of beer and cigarettes. Debra pays for the
items.

EXT. PARKING LOT

                  HOMELESS MAN
     Excuse me Ms.

Debra stops and looks at the homeless man

                  HOMELESS MAN
     Here is a rose for you. God told me
     to tell you he loves you and He has
     not forgotten about you.

                  DEBRA
        (smiles)
     Thank you

INT. DEBRA'S VEHICLE

Debra places the rose on the dashboard and her groceries in the passenger seat. She opens a beer, sits the can in the cupholder, lights a cigarette. She backs her vehicle out of the parking space and drives off.

Debra plays music and drinks from the open can of beer as she drives on the highway. When Debra finishes her beer, she lowers her window and throws out the empty beer can. Debra opens another and throws it oout the window when the can is empty.

Debra pulls over at a rest.

EXT. REST STOP

Debra gets out of vehicle,opens the back door and lets her dog out of the vehicle. Debra sits in the grass and talks to God.

                  DEBRA
     Okay God, I know you would not put
     anything on me that I could not
     bear. I know I got this. I am
     starting allover with no job and
     very little money.

Debra whistles for her dog and the dog came running. Debra opens the door to the backseat and the dog jumps in the backseat of the vehicle. Debra closes the door and opens the driver's side door. She gets into the car and the engine starts up. Debra's vehicle drives away.

INT. DEBRA'S VEHICLE

Debra turns her radio on. She opens a beer and lights a cigarett.

Debra arrives at new place, parks her vehicle, gets out of the car and walks into the office to get the keys to her new apartment. Debra gets back into her vehicle and drives to her apartment.

EXT. OUTSIDE OF VEHICLE

                DEBRA
         (stretches)

Christiana drives up and parks her vehicle next to Debra's vehicle. She gets out of her vehicle. Debra and Christiana embrace with a hug.

                CHRISTIANA
    Oh my, you have a dog. My allergies are going to kick in, and why do you smell like a bar. Have you been drinking and driving?

                DEBRA
    Yes.

                CHRISTIANA
    Your healing is not in that bottle. God is the answer for everything and with Him, you will never be alone. You are always in and out of relationships and you need to learn how to be alone.

Christiana grabs Debra's suitcase. Moving truck arrives.

INT. APARTMENT KITCHEN

Debra and Christiana sit at the kitchen table. Two plates are on the table in front of them. Christiana holds a fork in her hand and shovels the food left on her plate onto the fork. She places the fork in her mouth and chews.

                DEBRA
    I need to go back to church

                CHRISTIANA
    There are lots of churches out there. Pick one.

                DEBRA
    Yes, I know and eventually I will find one. Christiana, I am scared. This is the first time I have been by myself in seven years. I mean I have been with other people, but there has never been a break in between relationships.

                CHRISTIANA
    You got this friend, God got you. I've been by myself for years and I enjoy cooking for myself and taking myself out on dates.

                DEBRA
    I don't know if I can do that

                         CHRISTIANA
               Once you learn to enjoy yourself
               and get closer to God, everything
               else will fall into place.

Debra rolls her eyes and looks down at her phone. She is on a
dating site page.

                         CHRISTIANA
               You should get on the prayer line I
               just started calling into. It is
               every Wednesday and Friday at
               5:30am

                         DEBRA
               Okay, I will look into it. Send me
               the link.

                         CHRISTIANA
               Thanks for dinner, I'm going to
               head out. I just wanted to check on
               you to make sure you were okay.

EXT. OUTSIDE APARTMENT

Debra and Christiana hug. Christiana gets into her vehicle
and drives off.

Debra walks back to her apartment.

INT. APARTMENT BEDROOM - NIGHT

While Debra is lying in bed, she receives a notification on
her phone from an online dating site from a woman named
Luci. Debra and Luci start to message one another.

                         LUCI (V.O.)
                  Hello beautiful.

                         DEBRA (V.O.)

               Hello, how are you doing?

                         LUCI (V.O.)
               I'm doing well. Can we meet?

                         DEBRA (V.O.)
               yes, when?

                         LUCI (V.O)
                 How does tomorrow sound?

                         DEBRA (V.O)
               Tomorrow sounds great. Let's meet
               up at the spot called The Bar.

Debra puts her phone in the nightstand drawer, covers her dog up, and gets into bed.

While Debra is asleep the camera zooms in on the time. At 3:00 am the camera zooms out to Debra who is now awake. Debra kicks her blanket off in a tantrum, gets up, grabs a cigarette, and goes to the refrigerator to get a beer. Debra puts leash on the dog.

EXT. OUTSIDE

>   DEBRA
>   (walking her dog and
>   talking to herself,
>   laughs out loud and then
>   throws her beer can on
>   the ground)Maliah got me
>   messed up,

Debra goes back upstairs into apartment

INT. BEDROOM

Debra takes the leash off of her dog and goes back to bed.

INT. BEDROOM - MORNING

Debra's alarm clock goes off and she wakes up and turns alarm clock off.

Debra gets in the shower and and goes back to her bedroom to get dressed. While getting dressed, Debra receives a phone call.

INTERCUT PHONE CONVERSATION

Kathy sits at a desk in an office.

>   KATHY
>   Hello, this is Kathy from human
>   resource. I am calling in regards
>   to a job you applied for. If you
>   are still interested in the job, I
>   would like to schedue an interview.
>
>   DEBRA
>   Yes, I am still interested in the
>   job.

Debra writes down the day and time of the interview.

>   DEBRA
>   I got it. Thank you.

Debra hangs up the phone.

Debra grabs her purse and keys, and her phone rings.

                    DEBRA
              (Into phone)
          Hello?

                    MALIAH
          Hello, can I pick the dog up today?

                    DEBRA
          What time?

                    MALIAH
          I would like to come now.

Debra gives Maliah her address. 10 minutes later Maliah
arrives and picks the dog up.

Debra gets ready to got to The Bar. Debra leaves the house

                                        CUT TO:

INT. THE BAR- NIGHT

                    DEBRA
          I'd like to order a dirty martini
          and a beer.

Luci walks up and sits next to Debra.

                    LUCI
          You must be Debra. Hello, I am
          Luci, you look just like your
          picture.

                    DEBRA
          Hello, it is nice meet you.

                    LUCI
          What kind of work do you do?

                    DEBRA
          I am currently unemployed but have
          an interview in a few days.

                    LUCI
          What kind of work?

                    DEBRA
          That is not important. I just want
          to hang out and have fun.

Debra and Luci are at the bar talking, listening to music,
dancing, taking shots of liquor and drinking beer until The
Bar closed.

EXT. OUTSIDE OF THE BAR

                  LUCI
Would you like to end the night at my place?

                  DEBRA
Yes, I'll follow you to your place.

                  LUCI
Okay

Debra and Luci get into their vehicles and drive off.

INT. DEBRA'S VEHICLE

Debra folows behind Luci. Debra makes a sharp turn and her phone falls on the floor of the car on the driver's side. She bends down to pick it up, losing sight of the road for some time. Meanwhile, Luci turns down another street. Debra looks up and Luci is gone.

                  DEBRA
            (puzzling look on her
             face and widening her
             eyes)
Where did she go?

Debra stop vehicle and falls asleep.

Debra wakes up in vehicle in front of apartment.

Debra calls Christiana as she is walking up stairs.

INT. HOME

Christiana answers the phone.

INTERCUT PHONE CONVERSATION

                  DEBRA
Christiana, let me tell you about last night.

                  CHRISTIANA
Don't tell me, you got online after I left and you met someone.

                  DEBRA
Yes and yes.

                  CHRISTIANA
I told you not to get online. You have to get to know yourself and God.

DEBRA
I know, you did tell me to take time for myself. Luci and I met up at The Bar, afterwards I called myself following her home, but in the midst of following her I got lost and ended up waking up in my vehicle here at my place.

CHRISTIANA
That's what you get. I am glad you are safe and did not hurt yourself or anyone else while drinking and driving. You need to chill with the drinking and driving. You are becoming a loose canon.

DEBRA
I am fine and so is everyone else on the road. I drive better and much more cautious when I am drunk.

CHRISTIANA
(shakes her head and then puts her head in her hand)
Why don't you come down for a visit and we can go to church.

DEBRA
Hmmm, nah, I'm probably going to be too busy.

CHRISTIANA
Too busy for God?

DEBRA
He was too busy for me, and didn't warn me when Maliah broke my heart.

CHRISTIANA
You can't blame God for your decision on making bad choices.

DEBRA
Well, I will talk to you later. I need to prepare myself for the interview.

Debra hangs up the phone.

CHRISTIANA
(looks at the phone in shock)
Oh no, she did not.
(looks up at the ceiling)Lord, I pray that you keep her protected and safe.

EXT. OUTSIDE

Debra walks outside, singing. Constance hears.

CONSTANCE
Debra, is that you?

DEBRA
(Looks downstairs) Constance, is that you? Come up.

Constance walks upstairs.

CONSTANCE
Where have you been and how have you and Maliah been doing?

DEBRA
(Debra pats the seat for
Constance to sit)
Sit down

CONSTANCE
Thanks. You want an snow cone

DEBRA
Sure. Thank you

EXT. PARK

Constance and Debra walks to get a snow cone and then goes back to sit on the bench.

CONSTANCE
It has been a while.

DEBRA
I know. I just moved back to the City

CONSTANCE
Since when? And where is Maliah?

DEBRA
I left Maliah because she cheated on me.

CONSTANCE
I'm sorry. Hey, I attend church, you are more than welcome to come with me as my guest.

DEBRA
Okay.

CONSTANCE
(looks down at her phone
with no expression)
I am texting you the name, address
and time church starts.

DEBRA
See you Sunday. And it was great
seeing you.

Debra and Contstance hug and walk separate ways. Debra calls Christiana.

INTERCUT PHONE CONVERSATION

DEBRA
Hey, what are you doing?

CHRISTIANA
Getting ready to brush my teeth

DEBRA
Okay, well I ran into Constance and
she invited me to church.

CHRISTIANA
Praise God. I hope you said, yes.

Debra and Christiana both laugh

DEBRA
Of course I said, yes. Well I love
you I need to get ready for this
interview tomorrow.

CHRISTIANA
You got this. The job is already
yours.

DEBRA
Why do you have so much faith in
me? Christiana, did I ever tell
you, I told Mailiah I looked as
though she was my forever, and she
said, she never looked at me as her
forever. It stung, but she is not
my forever and I should never look
at any one other than God as my
forever.

CHRISTIANA
You are right!!!Come on God!!

INT. INSIDE APARTMENT

Debra wakes up at 3:00am and gets bible out of her closet and looks around for a pen and paper. Instead she finds a dry erase marker and writes a bible verse on the refrigerator.

                    DEBRA
               (Talking out loud)
          Jeremiah 29:11, for I
          know the plans I have
          for you declares the
          Lord, plans to prosper
          you and not to harm you.
          plans to give you hope
          and future.

Debra goes back to bed.

INT. APARTMENT- MORNING

Debra wakes up and walks into the kitchen to start a pot of coffee. She goes to her bedroom to get dressed. Debra kneels down at the side of her bed and prays.

                    DEBRA
               (Prays: Lord, I know I
          have not been at my
          best, but can you please
          show me some grace,
          favor and mercy. I need
          this job Amen)

Debra gets up from her kneeling position and puts her shoes on, grabs her bag. She turns off the stove, pours coffee into a to-go mug and leaves out of the door. As Debra is locking her door she sees her next door neighbor also leaving out.

EXT. OUTSIDE APARTMENT

                    DEBRA
               (smiles)
          Hello. My name is Debra.

                    CHANTRELLE
          My name is Chantrelle. Nice to meet
          you.

Debra walks downstais and gets into her vehicle.

INT. OFFICE - MORNING

Debra arrives at her interview and goes into a room. Debra comes out of the room and shakes the interviewer's hand and leaves.

Debra gets into vehicle and drives to her apartment. While walking upstairs she runs into her neighbor, who was looking over the banister.

EXT. OUTSIDE APARTMENT

CHANTRELLE
I was hoping to run into you. Would you like to go to a poetry spot with me tonight, if you're not busy.

DEBRA
Yes, I'd love to go. What time?

CHANTRELLE
I'll knock on your door in 30 minutes.

DEBRA
Okay.

INT. APARTMENT - NIGHT

Debra walks into her apartment, takes her shoes off and puts her bags down. She walks into the kitchen and opens up a beer. Debra sits on the sofa and drinks beer.

Debra goes to her bedroom and puts on an orange and outfit and throws her silk scarf around her neck. Debra kneels to the side of her bed to pray.

DEBRA
Lord, I know this is not the life you have planned for me. I am so exhausted. I have nothing else to do but go out. please keep me protected from any hurt, harm or danger.

Debra puts on her shoes. Debra and Chantrelle walks out of their doors at the same time.

DEBRA
I will meet you at the Poetry Spot.

CHANTRELLE
Okay, sounds good. You know you can ride with me.

DEBRA
I appreciate that. I'll drive so that I can leave when I'm ready to go. Can I follow you there.

CHANTRELLE
Okay.

INT. POETRY SPOT

Inside of the poetry spot there are four tables and there are four people at each table. There is a stage with a microphone, a DJ stand and a bar.

> FRIEND #1
> (waving at Chantrelle)
> Hey girl, we're over here.

> CHANTRELLE
> (waves back)
> Come on Debra that's one of my friend's

Chantrelle grabs Debra's hand and walks toward friend #1.

> DEBRA
> Okay, I'm coming

> CHANTRELLE
> Hey, how are you doing. This is my neighbor, Debra

> FRIEND #1
> I'm doing good girl. I am happy to see you.
> (Pause, stare and point to Debra and then rolls her eyes)
> Let me get you a drink

> CHANTRELLE
> You want a drink?

> DEBRA
> Sure, I'd take a beer, and a peppermint shot.

Chantrelle Goes to get drinks as Debra sits down next to friend #1.

> POET
> (Muffled voice)

Everyone in the audience has their hands up in the air, snapping their fingers. The poet is still on stage speaking, but you cannot hear them.

> CHANTRELLE
> Debra, this is Sally. Sally, Debra. Sally, what time did you get here.

> SALLY
> Maybe about 10 minutes before you.

Debra, Sally and Chantrelle are talking and laughing.

SALLY
Well cheers to us all ladies

Debra, Sally and Chantrelle clinked glasses and continued to drink.

DEBRA
Well ladies, I am going to call it a night. Sherry thank you for inviting me out to poetry night and maybe next time I am out I may spit out a little something, something.

SHERRY
You write poetry?

DEBRA
Nah. Good night.

Sally and Sherry waves good night and continue talking and drinking.

INT. APARTMENT

Debra walks into her home. Drops purse on the ground and takes shoes off by the door. Walks to her bedroom and changes into her bed clothes. Climbs into bed and covers herself up.

CUT TO:

INT. DEBRA'S DREAM

Debra went into her home. Drops purse on the ground and

takes shoes off by the door. Walks to her bedroom and changes into her bed clothes. Climbs into bed and covers herself up.

CUT TO:

INT. DEBRA'S DREAM - DAY

Debra went out to eat with a man and after dinner the unknown male and Debra were riding in a vehicle. Debra's lips started to swell. The unknown male kept driving straight and Debra and the unknown male never reached their destination.

CUT TO:

Debra wakes up at 3:00am, sits up in bed and looks over at the clock. Debra kneels down next to the bed.

                        DEBRA
             Our Father who art in
             heaven hallowed be thy
             name, thy kingdom come.
             Thy will be done in
             earth, as it is in
             heaven. Give us this day
             our daily bread. And
             forgive us our
             trespasses, as we
             forgive those who
             trespass against us. And
             lead us not into
             temptation, but deliver
             us from evil. For thine
             is the kingdom, the
             power and the glory
             forever and ever. Amen.
             (NIV Bible, Matthew
             6:9-13)

Debra gets back into bed and falls back to sleep.

INT. BEDROOM - DAY

Debra wakes up, goes to the bathroom to shower and then gets dressed for church. Debra wears a blue outfit.

INT. KITCHEN

Debra goes to the kitchen and starts coffee pot, gets dry erase marker and write on refrigerator.

                        DEBRA
                  (As Debra is writing on
                   the refrigerator, she is
                   talking out loud)
             Dream, unknown male,
              swollen lip that would
              not go down, driving and
              never reaching my
              destination. Hmmm,
              translation: I was with
              the wrong guy.
             Connection: I was unable
              to reach my destination
              because the guy was
              leading me down a
              destination I should not
              have been going.

Debra leaves the house.

INT. CHURCH

Debra walks inside of The Church and finds a seat.

Debra sings, closes her eyes, and raise her hands to God. Once the song is finished everyone holds hands to pray.

After the service, Constance walks over to Debra and hugs her.

> CONSTANCE
> You wanna have lunch?

> DEBRA
> Yes

> CONSTANCE
> Follow me

> DEBRA
> Okay

EXT. OUTSIDE OF CHURCH

Constance and Debra gets inside of their vehicles and leaves the church. They both walk into the restaurant at the same time, and sit down at a table. The waiter takes their drink orders.

> DEBRA
> I'd like to order a beer

> CONSTANCE
> You can get me water please.

The waiter walks away

> CONSTANCE
> How did you like the church service?

> DEBRA
> It was good and hit home. I know I need God's grace, mercy and favor. It felt good being back in church after nine years.

> CONSTANCE
> I'm glad you enjoyed it. I hope you come back.

> DEBRA
> I will.

> CONSTANCE
> So, now tell me about you and Maliah. Are you two getting back together?

DEBRA
(Debra widens her eyes
and straightens her
posture)
Oh, no!!

CONSTANCE
Have you spoken to her since you left?

DEBRA
She called me to pick up the dog.

CONSTANCE
Have you gotten into any counseling?

DEBRA
For what?

CONSTANCE
To talk to someone about the break up. Sometimes our past traumas dictates our current behaviors.

DEBRA
Constance, I will be okay. I don't need to talk to anyone. All I can say is that I am better now that I have moved away from her and I will never forgive her.

CONSTANCE
One day you'll forgive her.

DEBRA
I don't even know what that looks like.

Waiter brings drinks. The waiter takes their order for food and leaves.

DEBRA
I don't think I have gone a day without a drink in a very long time. Cheers

DEBRA AND CONSTANCE
(laughs and clinks
glasses)

Constance and Debra's character fades out as they are talking, but cannot be heard. After a while the waiter returns with food. Debra and Constance eat and enjoy one another's company.

                    DEBRA
            (phone rings and she
             answers)
Hello

                    CHRISTIANA
Hey, how are you doing?

                    DEBRA
I am doing well. Right now I am
having lunch with Constance. I'll
call you back once I get hone.

                    CHRISTIANA
Okay. Sounds good

Christiana and Debra hangs up

                    DEBRA
Okay Constance, I am going to head
out. I have work tomorrow. We are
definitely going to have to get
together again very soon.

                    CONSTANCE
Yes, it was great seeing you. See
you soon.

EXT. APARTMENT - NIGHT

Debra arrives home and walks into her place, puts her things
down and takes her shoes off at the door. Debra walks to her
bedroom. Debra gets ready for bed and then calls Christiana.

                    DEBRA
Hey girl, how are you doing?

                    CHRISTIANA
I'm doing well. Whatcha up to?

                    DEBRA
I went to church this morning.

                    CHRISTIANA
Praise God. How was it?

                    DEBRA
It was great being back in church.
The pastor spoke from Colossians
3:12-15.

                    CHRISTIANA
Okay. "Therefore as God's chosen
people, holy and dearly loves,
clothe yourselves with compassion,
kindness, humility, gentleness and
                    (MORE)

CHRISTIANA (cont'd)
patience. Bear with each other and forgive one another if any of you has a grievance against someone. Forgive as the Lord forgave you. And over all these virtues put on love which binds them all together in perfect unity, let the peace of Christ rule in your hearts, since as members of one body you were called to peace. And be thankful.

DEBRA
He spoke about putting God first and everything else will fall into place. Show people grace and love, and just because you have on church clothes does not mean you are a follower of God.

CHRISTIANA
That sounds about right. Amen.

DEBRA
I want that, but I don't know how. Oh, I forgot to tell you I got the job. I start tomorrow. I am getting ready to turn these light out. I love you.

CHRISTIANA
I knew the job was yours. We will talk tomorrow. Good night love.

DEBRA
Good night.

Debra turns light out.

FADE TO BLACK

INT. APARTMENT - DAY

Debra wakes up and goes to the kitchen and turns on teh coffee pot. She walks back to room and gets dressed or work, brush teeth and walks back to kitchen to fix lunch.

Debra's phone rings. Debra answers the phone.

INTERCUT PHONE CONVERSATION

CHRISTIANA
Good morning. I wanted to wish you a great first day at work.

                    DEBRA
          Thank you friend. I will call you
          after I get off to let you know how
          my firs day went.

                    CHRISTIANA
          Sounds good.

Debra and Christiana hangs up.

Debra gather her things for work and then walks to the
kitchen to get coffee and lunch. Debra leaves out the door.

INT. WORKPLACE - DAY

Debra arrives at the office.

                    CO-WORKER
          Hello, my name is Dewon. I was
          asked to show you around. Oh, I
          also need to get your phone number.
          We all have each other's phone
          numbers in case of emergencies

                    DEBRA
              (Debra wrinkles forehead
               with a puzzling look on
               her face)
          Okay.

Debra writes her phone number on a piece of paper. Dewon
shows Debra around the office.

                    DEWON
          You can take the rest of the day
          off since the boss isn't here
          today. They just asked me to show
          you around your office.

                    DEBRA
              (rolls her eyes)
          Oh and ask for my phone number.

EXT. HOME

Debra walks into her home and receives text messages from
Dewon.

                    DEWON (V.O)
          Hey, it was nice meeting
          you and see you at work
          tomorrow. Oh, I have a
          question.

                    DEBRA (V.O)
               What's your question?

                    DEWON (V.O)
               Would you like to come
               over to my place
               tonight?

                    DEBRA (V.O)
               No thank you.

                    DEWON (V.O)
               I like you and I will
               cook for you.

                    DEBRA (V.O)
               You don't even know me
               and I don't know you.

                    DEWON (V.O)
               Dewon have you looked at
               me?

                    DEBRA (V.O)
               LOL, I looked at you and
               again, I don't know you)

Debra puts her phone in her nightstand drawer, climbs into bed and goes to sleep.

                                        FADE TO BLACK

INT. OFFICE- DAY

                    DEWON
               Good morning, Debra.

                    DEBRA
               Good morning.

Debra puts her things down in her office and sits down at her desk. Dewon comes into Debra's office.

                    DEWON
               Can I take you on a date tonight?

                    DEBRA
               No. Can you leave my office. I have
               work to do.

Dewon leaves Debra's office. Debra looks down and continues to work.

                    DEWON
               (peeks around the door)
          Can I take you out on a date
          tonight?

                    DEBRA
               (sighs out loud)
          You never give up do you. Okay. I
          will meet you at The Spot after
          work.

INT. THE SPOT - NIGHT

Debra walks into The Spot.

Debra looks around and sees Dewon. Debra walks towards
Dewon. Dewon pulls chair out for Debra. Debra and Dewon
order and eat dinner

                    DEBRA
          Thanks for inviting me. I am
          getting ready to head home.

                    DEWON
          Thanks for coming. You sure you
          don't want to end with a night cap?

                    DEBRA
          My idea of a night cap is a cup of
          tea in my pajamas. You have a good
          night.

                    DEWON
          Hahaha. You too.

Debra gets up and leaves The Spot.

INT. NIGHT. HOME

Debra arrives home and walks inside of her home, takes her
shoes off and puts her purse down at the door. Debra goes to
refrigerator and pulls out four beers. She sits at the table
and drinks the four beers. She receive a text message from
Dewon.

                    DEWON (V.O)
          Would you like to meet me
           for coffee in the
           morning at this coffee
           shop called, The Best
           Coffee?

                    DEBRA (V.O)
          What time?

                    DEWON (V.O)
          At 9:00am

                    DEBRA (V.O)
          Sure.

INT. BEDROOM - NIGHT

Debra walks to bedroom and changes clothes and goes to bed.

                                        FADE TO BLACK

INT. BEST COFFEE SHOP - DAY

Debra enters The Best Coffeee shop and orders coffee and sits at a table.

Debra looks at her watch and 20 minutes has passed. She receives a text message from Dewon.

                    DEWON (V.O)
          How is your coffee?

                    DEBRA (V.O)
          I think you have issues
           and by the way my coffee
          was great

                    DEWON (V.O)
          Come over to my place.

                    DEBRA (V.O)
          Give me your address.

EXT. OUTSIDE DEWON'S HOUSE

Debra gets out of her vehicle, walks to the door and knocks on Dewon's door.

                    DEBRA
          Hey, Dewon are you there.

INTERCUT PHONE CONVERSATION

                    DEWON
          Hello?

                    DEBRA
          Hey, where are you? I am here at
          your house per your invite.

                    DEWON
          I'm not there, I'm at my friend's
          house.

                    DEBRA
          Why would you ask me to come over
          if you already had plans.

                    DEWON
          You can stay there and I'll be
          there in an hour.

                    DEBRA
          Nah, I'm good

Debra hangs up the phone.

Debra rears back and gets ready to kick the door in. She
then walks up to the door and jingles the doorknob. The door
is unlocked. Debra opens the door wider and walks inside.
She closes the door behind her.

                    DEBRA
          What an idiot. Who keeps their door
          unlocked for strangers to enter?

Debra opens the refrigerator and freezer door. She takes
items out of the refrigerator and freezer drops them on the
floor. Debra goes into the bathroom and puts a stopper in
the tub drainage and turns on the hot water. Debra goes to
the kitchen sink, puts the stopper in the sink and turns the
water on. On Debra's way out of Dewon's house she cranks the
heater up.

                    DEBRA
               (walks out of the door
                confident and smug)
          That will teach him.

EXT. OUTSIDE DEBRA'S APARTMENT

Debra walking upstairs to her home. Chantrelle was sitting
next door at a table.

                    CHANTRELLE
          Hey Debra, you want a beer?

                    DEBRA
          Of course.

Debra's phon rings. It is Dewon. Debra answer's the call
from Dewon and puts it on speaker.

                    DEWON (V.O)
          Were you at my place?

                    DEBRA (V.O)
          Why would you ask me that?

                    DEWON (V.O)
          Because someone came into my place
          and flooded it. It is a mess in
          here. Good thing I have cameras.

                    DEBRA
          Well if you have cameras, you would
          see who flooded your place.

Debra hangs up the phone. Chantrelle and Debra open their
beers. Debra lets out a low toned evil chuckle.

                    CHANTRELLE
          I got a question for ya.

                    DEBRA
          Shoot.

                    CHANTRELLE
          Did you do it?

                    DEBRA
               (debra gives a side ways
                smile and chuckles)
          If I tell you, I might have to kill
          you.

Debra and Sherry laugh out loud and clink beers.

                    DEBRA
          I have a question for you.

                    CHANTRELLE
          Shoot.

                    DEBRA
          Are you dating anyone? I have never
          seen anyone leave your place at
          weee hours of the morning.

                    CHANTRELLE
          It's complicated.

                    DEBRA
               (looks down at her watch
                and tilts her head and
                looks at Sherry)
          I have nothing but time.

                    CHANTRELLE
               (laughs out loud)
          I have been on and off with someone
          for a very long time.

DEBRA
(Debra drags her words)
So, right now is it off or on?

SHERRY
I don't know. She is complicated.

DEBRA
(Debra takes shoes off
and puts purse on the
table as she continues
to drink her beer)
Tell me about it. Talk to me girl.

CHANTRELLE
Have you ever been with someone who only wants you around when it's convenient for them. Well that's her. I know she really doesn't want to be with me, but when she wants me around it makes me feel good and wanted.

DEBRA
That does not sound complicated, it sounds like she is using you.

SHERRY
Yeah, that pretty much sums it up.

Debra and Chantrelle clink beers. Chantrelle reaches in her pocket and takes out a stone and sits it on the table.

DEBRA
What is that? Well I mean I know what it is, but why are you carrying a stone in your pocket?

CHANTRELLE
I carry it for different reason. I carry this one for energy and focus.

DEBRA
Why carry a stone when God can be with you wherever you go? I still believe even though I have been feeling empty for a long time. I want to get to a place of fulfillment.

CHANTRELLE
I don't believe there is a God. If I can control my reality and what happens to me, then I am God!

                    DEBRA
          A person's behavior dictates their
          reality. So, if I decide to drink
          and drive. I create my reality of
          getting a DUI. I must say you're
          something else. You worship stones,
          you don't believe in God. Can I ask
          what you do believe in, King
          Nebuchadnezzar?

                    CHANTRELLE
          I have a statue that I pray to.

Debra gets her bible out of her purse and turns to Exodus.

                    DEBRA

          Well according to the B-I-b-l-e,
          Exodus 20:3-4, "Thou shalt have no
          other Gods before me. Thou shalt
          not make unto thee any graven
          image, or any likeness of anything
          that is in heaven above, or that is
          in the earth beneath, or that is
          under the water under the earth".
          Oh, wait, Exodus 23:13, "Be careful
          to do everything I have said to
          you. Do not invoke the names of
          other Gods; do not let them be
          heard on your lips, which is one of
          the Sabbath laws".

                    CHANTRELLE
          I believe what I belive, and you
          believe what you believe.

Chantrelle pours she and Debra and herself another shot and
opens two more beers. Sherry places one beer in front of
Debra.

                    CHANTRELLE
          Drink up.

Debra and Chantrelle continue talking and laughing but it is
muted.

                    CHANTRELLE
          I like you.

                    DEBRA
          I like you too. Just because we
          have different beliefs does no mean
          I like you any different from
          anyone else.

CHANTRELLE
(nods her head up and
down and smiles)
I appreciate that. Can I ask you a question?

DEBRA
Of course.

SHERRY
Are you into women?

DEBRA
I used to be in a seven year relationship with a woman, but not anymore.

SHERRY
Okay. Why not?

DEBRA
(shrugs her shoulder)
Eh. Right now I am not interested in anyone. I am trying to find my way back to God, but I keep falling back into sinning.

SHERRY
Isn't your God a forgiving God.

DEBRA
He is and don't be mockin' Him.

CHANTRELLE
Okay, believer. How does it look in God's eye when you messed up your co workers place.

DEBRA
I am not perfect, and didn't you hear me say, I want to find my way back to God, but I keep sinning. Shut up and pour me another shot.

CHANTRELLE
(glares at Debra and
smiles)
You shut up and drink up!!

DEBRA
Oh, and about my co worker's place. All I have to say is, check the camera to see who flooded his place.

Debra and Sherry both laugh out loud and clink beer bottles, and then they down their beer and slam their empty beer bottles on the table.

                    DEBRA
          Well, Sherry, it is past my
          bedtime. Thank you for the
          conversation and I will talk to you
          tomorrow

Debra stands up and walks up to Chantrelle. She gives her a hug and a kiss on the cheek. Debra walks into her apartment.

INT. APARTMENT - NIGHT

Debra goes into the refrigerator and grabs two beers, and walks to her room

                                         FADE TO BLACK

INT. OFFICE - DAY

Debra arrives at work and walks into her office,Debra sits at her desk and a client knocks on her door.

                    CLIENT
          Can I talk to you

                    DEBRA
          Sure, come on in and have a seat.

                    DEWON
          I need to talk to you, can you talk
          to him in a minute

                    DEBRA
              (To client)
          I apologize, do you mind waiting
          for just a moment? And could you
          please close my door behind you?

Client leaves the office and closes the door

                    DEWON
              (calls Debra)
          What are you doing later?

                    DEBRA
          I'm busy. So do do not call me and
          ask me to hang out with you after
          work. You are very disrespectful,
          rude and inconsiderate. Dude, you
          called me to have coffee and then
          had the nerve to say you were at
          your friend's house after inviting
          me over to your place.

                    DEWON
          I'm sorry

                    DEBRA
          Yea, you are. From this moment on,
          I will handle you accordingly.

Dewon leaves Debra's office. The client enters the office.

                                        CUT TO:

INT. OFFICE - NIGHT

Debra shuts her computer down, grabs her purse and starts walking out of her office. Dewon stands near the doorway. Debra closes her door and walks around him.

                                        FADE OUT

INT. GROCERY STORE - NIGHT

Debra walks into the grocery store and receives a call from her mom.

                    DEBRA
          (phone rings and takes
           her phone out of her
           purse to answer it)
          Hello (pause)
          How many sweet potatoes
           do you want me to get?
          (pause)
          Okay.

                    DEBRA
          (walks up to the produce
           guy)
          Do you guys have any sweet
          potatoes?

                    PRODUCE GUY
          No, we are all out. If you give me
          your number, I can call you when
          they come in.

                    DEBRA
          (laughs out loud)
          You know what, I think I'm gonna
          entertain this. Give me your phone.

Debra types in her number. She hands the produce Guy his phone back. Debra walks away. The produce guy stares at her as she walks away.

                    PRODUCE GUY
          (text: You are beautiful.
           See you soon)

                    DEBRA
          (Text: Thank you. Don't
          forget to let me know
          when those sweet
          potatoes arrive)

                                        FADE OUT

INT. HOME

Debra gets a 6 pack of beer out of her refrigerator and
walks to her room, sits on her bed and turns the light outs.
The audio hears Debra opening up a beer.

                                        FADE TO BLACK

INT. BEDROOM - DAY

There are beer cans all over Debra's bedroom floor. She
picks them up and puts them into a trash bag and then lies
back down.

                    DEBRA
          I am not going to even try to make
          it to work. I am still feeling a
          little drunk.

                    DEBRA (V.O)
          Hello, I am not going to be in
          today. I am not feeling well.

                    WORK
          Okay, I hope you get to
          feeling better.

Debra goes back to sleep

Debra wakes up to a text mesaage

                    PRODUCE GUY
          (text: hello, the sweet
          potatoes are here)

                    DEBRA
          (text: Thank you. I will
          be there to pick them up
          later today)

                    PRODUCE GUY
          (text: hello what time
          are you coming for the
          sweet potatoes?)

                    DEBRA
          (text: I will come now)

Debra out of bed, throws on sweats and grabs her keys and
leaves out of the house. Debra sees a woman walk out of

Sherry's place.

FADE IN:

INT. GROCERY STORE - DAY

Debra walks inside of the grocery store and is greeted by produce guy.

PRODUCE GUY
Hello, how many sweet potatoes do you want?

DEBRA
You can bag up seven sweet potatoes please.

Produce guys bags up the seven sweet potatoes.

DEBRA
Thank you.

PRODUCE GUY
You're welcome. Can I ask you something?

DEBRA
Sure
(starts to walk to the check out counter and Produce guys starts walking with her)

PRODUCE GUY
I know you don't know me, but

DEBRA
Spit it out, I really don't feel well.

PRODUCE GUY
Can I take you on a date?

DEBRA
Sure.

PRODUCE GUY
Great! How does tomorrow sound at 7:00pm?

DEBRA
Sounds good, where do I meet you?

PRODUCE GUY
Can I pick you up?

                    DEBRA
                (eyes widen)
          Oh, no. I will meet you at the
          location you give me.

                    PRODUCE GUY
          Can I text you with a location
          later today?

                    DEBRA
          Of course, sounds good. You enjoy
          the rest of your day.

As Debra walks away from produce guy, she turns around and
she sees him staring at her.

                    PRODUCE GUY
                (laughs and then waves
                 goodbye at Debra)

EXT. OUTSIDE APARTMENT BUILDING - DAY

Debra arrives home and gets out of vehicle, walks upstairs
and sees Sherry standing by her door drinking beer.

                    SHERRY
          Hey Debra, you want to join me for
          a couple of beers?

                    DEBRA
          Of course, let me put my things
          inside and I'll be right back

Debra opens her door and places her things inside of her
place and grabs a six pack of beer and her smokes.

Debra sits down at the table and chair set outside of
Sherry's door. Sherry's notebook is on the table.

                    DEBRA
          What's in the notebook

                    SHERRY
          Oh, this is private

                    DEBRA
          Well maybe you need to put your
          private up.

Debra and Sherry laughs

                    SHERRY
          I'm writing a novel about my life

                    DEBRA
                (nods her head)
          That is awesome.

DEBRA
A long time ago I wrote a children's book,called, "I can dress myself" Needless to say the manuscript was rejected.

SHERRY
Have you sent anything else in since then?

DEBRA
No.

SHERRY
Well then, how was your day?

DEBRA
My day was good. I met this guy who works at the grocery store. He thought he was slick and I was onto his game. I played along with it.

SHERRY
What did he say?

DEBRA
Well I went in for sweet potatoes and there weren't any. He asked for my phone number to call after they came in. First of all I knew he was hitting on me. I was like what the heck, he may be a little fun.

SHERRY
You are too much!

DEBRA
I like to have fun.

SHERRY
Too much fun can get you in trouble.

DEBRA
He asked me out on a date and I said, yes.

SHERRY
When is your date?

DEBRA
It's tomorrow at 7:00. Oh, I did see your girlfriend leaving your house this morning.

SHERRY
(laughs and holds her
phone down)
Well you know, I had a good night.

                    DEBRA
          Well, do tell.

                    SHERRY
          A lady never tells.

                    DEBRA
               (laughs)
          You are not a lady

                    SHERRY
          Hahahaha. Anyway, what do you have
          going on after your date?

                    DEBRA
          I will be over here telling you all
          about it.

                    SHERRY
          Right on.

                    DEBRA
               (looks at her watch)
          Hey, it is late, I have to go to
          bed. I have work in the morning.

                    SHERRY
          Okay, you have a good night. I'll
          clean this up

                    DEBRA
          Thank you

Debra walks over to Sherry. Sherry stands up and they hug one another.

                    SHERRY
          Good night.

                    DEBRA
          Good night

                                                  FADE OUT

INT. BEDROOM - NIGHT

Debra looks in her closet for something to wear. Debra grabs her phone and calls Sherry.

                    DEBRA
               (To phone)
          Hey, I need help finding something
          to wear for my date. Can you help
          me.

                    DEBRA
              (Afte a pause)
          The door is open.

Debra hangs up the phone. Sherry enters Debra's apartment.

                    SHERRY (O.S)
          Hey, where are you?

                    DEBRA
          I'm back here in my room.

Chantrelle walks into Debra's bedroom. Debra is lying on the bed.

                    SHERRY
          Girl, get up.

                    DEBRA
          Okay. Let me go pour us a glass of wine.

KITCHEN

Debra gets wine out of the refrigerator and two wine glasses out of the cabinet and pours them both a glass of wine.

                    DEBRA
              (hands Sherry her glass
               of wine)
          Here you go

                    SHERRY
              (takes glass of wine from
               Debra)
          Thank you.

                    DEBRA
              (takes a sip of her wine)
          Okay, help, what color should I wear?

                    SHERRY
          Here, wear these purple pants with these yellow heels and yellow scarf.

                    DEBRA
              (puts on clothes as
               Sherry hands them to
               her)
          Thank you, well I am getting ready to head out to this date.

                    SHERRY
          Stop by afterwards to tell me how it went.

                    DEBRA
          Okay, I will if it's not to late.

                    SHERRY
          Okay. Have fun

EXT. OUTSIDE APARTMENT - NIGHT

INT. BLUE CORN RESTAURANT

                                        FADE OUT

Debra walks inside. Produce guy stands up and waves to get Debra's attention.

Debra sees the produce guy and walks to the table. She gives produce guy a hug and says hello to the two people sitting at the table.

                    PRODUCE GUY
          Debra, these are my friend Kenny
          and Sarah.

                    DEBRA
          Hello. Nice to meet you.

Sarah and Kenny sit next to each other. Sarah leans up against Kenny and whispers into his ear, while staring at Debra

                    DEBRA
                (left elbow on the table
                 and head resting on
                 chin)
          Produce guy, why would you invite
          someone on a date with us? And why
          are your friends staring at me?

                    PRODUCE GUY
          It was supposed to be a date with
          just you and me, but when I was at
          work talking about you and taking
          you on a date, my friend suggested
          a double date and I just said okay.

                    DEBRA
                (whispers)
           Red flag number one.
                (aloud)
          It would havee been nice to have a
          heads up.

                    PRODUCE GUY
          I'm sorry

                    SARAH
          Debra, you look nice

                    DEBRA
            Thank you

                    PRODUCE GUY
                (leans over to Debra)
            Sarah and Kenny invited us to their
            house for dessert. Would you like
            to go? We don't have to stay long.

                    DEBRA
            Sure, why not

After eating everyone pays and leaves the restaurant.
Produce guy walks Debra to her vehicle.

                                        FADE OUT

                                        FADE IN:

EXT. OUTSIDE SARAH AND KENNY'S HOME - NIGHT

Debra stands outside of her vehicle as Produce guy drives
up. Debra and Produce guy walks up and knocks on the door,
while holding Debra's hand.

                    KENNY
            Come in. Sarah is in the kitchen
            getting drinks and dessert
            prepared.

INT. OUTSIDE SARAH AND KENNY'S HOME

Debra and produce guy walks inside the home, and sits on the
sofa. Kenny gives Debra and produce guy a glass of wone

                    KENNY
            My wife is in the kitchen getting
            dessert ready.

Sarah comes from out of the kitchen holding a apple pie,
plates and silverware. She sets the items onto the table.

                    SARAH
            Debra, would you like to
            see the backyard?

                    DEBRA
            Sure

BACKYARD

Debra and Sarah walk outside to the backyard and sits
underneath the tree at a patio table and chair set.

                    SARAH
            So, how did you meet produce guy?

                    DEBRA
          We met at the store in the produce
          section. I was looking for sweet
          potatoes and there weren't any. He
          asked for my number to call after
          the sweet potatoes came in.

                    SARAH
          I bet he called you before the
          sweet potatoes came in

                    DEBRA
          Of course he did. I wouldn't have
          expected anything less.

Sarah and Debra laugh out loud and clink glasses.

                    DEBRA
          How did you meet your husband?

                    SARAH
          I met him after he was released
          from jail. He was at the park
          fishing and I was at the park
          sitting on a bench reading a book.
          He walked over to me after I stood
          up.

                    DEBRA
          What did he go to jail for?

                    SARAH
          He went to jail for selling drugs
          but he is currently on probation.

                    DEBRA
          How long has he been out of jail?

                    SARAH
          He's been out for one year. If he
          gets in any trouble he will be sent
          back to jail.

Sarah stops mid sentence

                    SARAH
               (gazing into Debra's
                eyes)
          Can I tell you something?

                    DEBRA
          Of course.

                    SARAH
          You are beautiful and very
          attractive.

DEBRA
(puzzled look)
Thank you?

Debra takes a large gulp of her wine.

SARAH
I used to be with women before marrying my husband, and he aware. Well anyway after dinner as we were driving home tonight my husband and I were talking about how nice it would be to have you in our bed.

Debra spits her wine out.

DEBRA
Excuse me?

Debra puts her wine glass down, stand up and look at Sarah.

DEBRA
Sarah, I appreciate the compliment, but I have been delivered from homosexuality. I am not that person anymore.

Sarah stands up, takes Debra's hand and leans into kiss Debra.

Debra pushed Sarah back turns towards the house and sees Kenny staring at them through the kitchen window. Debra walks fast from the backyard into the house, grabs her bag and leaves.

PRODUCE GUY
Hey, where are you going?

DEBRA
I am going home. Your friend's wife made a pass at me, tried to kiss me, and you friend stood at the kitchen window watching. Where were you?

PRODUCE GUY
(Stammers)
I didn't know they were like that. I am sorry.

DEBRA
Don't call me anymore

Debra gets into her vehicle and drives off.

EXT. OUTSIDE OF DEBRA'S APARTMENT

Chantrelle sits in front of hr door.

                    DEBRA
          Hey girl, why are you out so late?

                    CHANTRELLE
          Girl, I decided to wait up for you
          just to make sure you made it home
          okay.

                    DEBRA
          The lies you tell. You want to know
          how the date went.

                    CHANTRELLE
          Oh yeah that too.

Debra and Sherry both laugh. Debra sits at the outside table
and opens a beer.

                    SHERRY
          So, how did the date go?

                    DEBRA
          Very interesting. First, the
          produce guy brings a couple so the
          date turned into a double date. At
          dinner the couple were staring at
          me, which made me feel
          uncomfortable. We went to their
          house after dinner for dessert.
          Girl, the wife, Sara thought I was
          going to be her dessert. Oh not to
          forget to mention, her husband as
          well. She tried to kiss me and he
          was watching from the kitchen
          window. It was creepy and I left.

Cdhantrelle opens another beer for Debra. Debra starts
drinking the beer in silence, stands up, puts the beer down
and grabs her things.

                    CHANTRELLE
          Where are you going?

                    DEBRA
          I'm going to change and then taking
          a ride.

Chantrelle Puts her things up into her apartment after Debra
walks into her apartment and sits at the table waiting for
Debra to come out of her apartment. Debra comes out of her
apartment.

                    DEBRA
          Hey girl, who are you waiting on?

                    SHERRY
          You, lets ride.

                          DEBRA
                Okay, I'm driving. You stay in the
                vehicle when we get to our
                destination.

                          SHERRY
                Okay, I'll try.

Sherry and Debra arrives at Sarah and Kenny's home.

Debra goes to her trunk and grabs a bag that appears to be heavy. Sherry seen her struggling with the bag and gets out of the vehicle to help.

                          SHERRY
                I know you told me to stay in the
                car, but you looked like you needed
                a little help.

                          DEBRA
                Yeah, thanks, help me carry it to
                the porch.

Sherry and Debra drags bag to the porch of Kenny and Sarah.

                          DEBRA
                Sherry, you might want to go back
                to the car.

                          SHERRY
                Nah, I want to see what you got in
                that bag.

Debra empties the bag on the porch and kicks the door really loud. Sherry ran and jumped into the car through the window of the back seat. Debra runs to the trunk and grabs a bat and then walks to Sarah and Kenny's vehicle.

Debra jump on top of their vehicle and then stands on the roof of Sarah and Kenny's vehicle.

                          CHANTRELLE
                     (whispers loudly)
                Girl, get off those people's car

Kenny opens door and steps outside and steps on road kill. He looks up and sees Debra standing on the roof of his vehicle. Sarah comes outside and slips and falls on the road kill.

                          KENNY
                Get off of my car

                          SARAH
                     (screams)
                I'm going to call the police

                          KENNY
                Hold up. Don't call the police

                    DEBRA
          You better not or else little old
          Kenny will be going back to lock up
          for a very long time.

Sarah is walking back and forth with her hands on her head mumbling.

                    SARAH
          Why are you doing this?

                    DEBRA
              (Points to Sarah)
          This will give you something to
          think about next time you decide to
          be disrespectful.

Debra points bat at Kenny.

                    DEBRA
              (angry and firm tone)
          And this will give you something to
          think about when you want to be
          nasty and watch from the window,
          you creeper.

Debra jumps from the roof of the car onto the hood of the vehicle, sits while tapping the bat against the headlight.

                    SARAH
              (Yells)
          Why are you doing this?

Debra gets back into her vehicle, where Sherry is kneels behind the back seat.

                    DEBRA
          Laughs out loud, get your scary
          self in the front

                    SHERRY
          Is the coast clear?

                    DEBRA
          Yes

Debra drives off after Sarah and Kenny walks inside their house. A vehicle behind Debra at the light flashes her with their high beams after she drives off.

                    CHANTRELLE
          Who is flashing you?

                    DEBRA
          Who knows

Debra continues driving and the flashing stops.

                                                  FADE OUT

EXT. OUTSIDE APARTMENT

DEBRA AND SHERRY
Good night.

INT. APARTMENT - NIGHT

Debra gets into the shower, writes on her refrigerator, "I am tired of drinking alcohol", prays and then goes to bed.

FADE OUT

INT. APARTMENT- DAY

Debra wakes up, gets dressed, pours a cup of coffee and go sit outside and reads her Bible. Daniel shows up at her place.

DEBRA
Oh my goodness, dude what do you have in your bag?

DANIEL
A beer for the both of us.

DEBRA
What kind?

DANIEL
Iron beer

DEBRA
I don't drink that kind and plus it is too early and I'm still drinking my coffee.

DANIEL
Like drinking in the morning ever stopped you before.

DEBRA
Hey, I am going inside to eat breakfast.

DANIEL
I seen you last night. I was flashing my light at you. What were you doing out so late?

DEBRA
You have a good day.

DANIEL
Can I come in, I have been drinking and one of my tail light is out.

DEBRA
You knew your taillight was out before you came out this way and no you cannot come in.

DANIEL
Did you hear the part about me drinking.

DEBRA
I didn't even open your beer. You cannot come in and have a good day.

Debra walks inside of her home. Daniel sits in Debra's chair outside of her home. Daniel opens his beer and props his feet up on her table.

SHERRY
Hey, who are you?

DANIEL
I am Debra's friend. I seen her and someone in her vehicle last night.

CHANTRELLE
(worried look on her face)
Where did you see us going?

DANIEL
Oh, you were I the car with her? I seen you guys at a traffic light.

CHANTRELLE
(relief and smiles)
Yes

DANIEL
So, what were you two doing out so late?

CHANTRELLE
(drinking a beer and looks up at Daniel while her mouth is still on her bottle)
Uhm, we were out grabbing beer.

DANIEL
Oh, okay. Can you tell Debra I said, bye?

CHANTRELLE
I sure will.

DANIEL
You and Debra just stay out of trouble.

CHANTRELLE
(puzzled look on her face and whispers under her breath)
I don't know what you mean by that, but okay.

Daniel gets in his car. Debra comes outside after Daniel drives off.

CHANTRELLE
Who is that guy?

DEBRA
I call him, The annoying one. I like him, but he aggravates me.

DEBRA
(takes a sip out of her coffee)
Can I ask you a question?

CHANTRELLE
Sure

DEBRA
Do you believe in God?

CHANRELLE
Uhm, no, I've said it before there is no God.

DEBRA
Why would you say that. There is a God.

CHANTRELLE
I am my own God.

DEBRA
I can't play with you anymore. What do you believe in?

SHERRY
I believe in, well let me show you.

Sherry takes Debra inside of her place where there is an altar next to a figurine. Debra looks at the altar, turn around and walks out of the door.

Debra sits down at the table set outside of Sherry's door. Sherry came outside and sat across from Debra.

SHERRY
Hey, I'm sorry I didn't know that would upset you

                    DEBRA
          I accept your apology. I think I am
          gonna go home. I'm sleepy and gotta
          gouge my eyes out from looking at
          that altar (hands pointing to eyes
          in a stabbing motion)

                    CHANTRELLE
          Okay, Okay don't talk about my
          altar. I don't talk about your God.

                    DEBRA
          Well you did, by putting another
          God before God. Well I am going
          home the darkness in your apartment
          made me sleepy.

                    SHERRY
          Oh, you got jokes

Debra and Sherry give each other a hug.

                    DEBRA AND SHERRY
          Good night.

INT. BEDROOM - NIGHT

Debra is in bed and falls asleep and has a dream

INTERCUT PHONE CONVERSATION

Debra visually sees this in her dreams, and it is acted out. Debra dreams of being at dinner with a black male and unable to see his face. Debra and the faceless male got into a vehicle after dinner. The male was driving and Debra's lip starts to swell. She puts chapstick on her lips and nothing she did would allow the swelling to go down. Debra puts on peppermint chapstick and oil on her lip. The faceless man kept driving and they never reached their destination.

Debra wakes up out of her sleep, looks at the clock that read 3:00am. Debra dangles her leg off the side of the bed. She gets her phone and calls Christiana.

NTERCUT PHONE CONVERSATION

                    DEBRA
          Hello

                    CHRISTIANA
               (sits up and picks up her
                phone)
          Hey girl, what time is it? Are you
          okay?

                    DEBRA
          Hey, I had a dream and the dream
          woke me up.

                    CHRISTIANA
          Make sure you write your dream
          down.

                    DEBRA
          I will. Well I know it is 3:00 in
          the morning and you are probably
          sleepy so I'm gonna let you go back
          to sleep.

                    CHRISTIANA
          Okay. I will talk to you later. Get
          you some rest.

                    DEBRA
          Will do.

Debra and Christiana hang up the phone.

Debra lies back in the bad and talks to Jesus.

                    DEBRA
          Jesus, I know that I fall short of
          your glory. I also know I drink a
          lot and I just want you to deliver
          me from alcoholism and bring my
          gifts to the forefront.

INT. BEDROOM - DAY

Debra wakes up and gets out of bed walks to her desk and takes a wipe erase marker out of the desk drawer.

KITCHEN

Debra walks into the kitchen starts brewing coffee. Then walks to the refrigerator and writes: Jeremiah 29:11. Debra walks to the bedroom and is quietly talking to God.

BEDROOM

She grabs her bible from her bedroom drawer and creates a prayer corner inside of her closet. Debra kneels to pray silently.

Debra comes out of her prayer closet and starts to get dressed to go out. Debra walks outside of her home.

                                        FADE IN:

INT. POETRY SPOT

Debra walks inside of the poetry club and walks up to the bar and orders two shots and two beers for herself. Debra takes a shot and places the shot glasss on the counter. She picks up the other shot glass and the two beers. Debra walks around to find a table. Once she finds one, she sits down and then place her two beers and shot on the table.

DJ Mike speaks out of the microphone

> DJ MIKE
> I would like to welcome you a The poetry Club. If you want to spit some poetry tonight the sign up sheet is in the back of the room. Everyone, welcome Chantrelle back to the stage.

> SHERRY
> I once knew who God was, but through influences I lost sight of Him. You say your God, I say I am God. I hold the Rod. The Rod you ask. It is the Rod to the destiny I create.

> DJ MIKE
> Thank you Sherry. That was dark. Girl, I am going to pray for you.

> DJ MIKE
> I would now like to introduce Kari to the stage.

> KARI
> The life you live can make, break or destroy you. My life was far from the eye of you know my mighty, heavenly father. He has different names. Jireh, Jehovah, God, my Lord and yes many more. My journey was not living for my God and that is the name I am going to use, while I recite this message to you. My confessions are dark you see. From sex, drugs, manipulation and deceit. I was living everything opposite of the fruit of the spirit, which is love, joy, peace, kindness, goodness, faithfulness, gentleness, self control and forbearance.

The camera is on Debra while she is drinking her beer and wiping the tears from her eyes. Debra stands up and walks to the back of the room to continue to listen to poetry.

> DEBRA
> Hello, what is your name

> GIRL
> My name is Cynthia

                    DEBRA
          What do you have going on later
          tonight?

                    CYNTHIA
          Whatever you have going on.

                    DEBRA
          I can follow you to your place.

                    CYNTHIA
          Okay, are you ready?

Debra downs her beer and takes her last shot of liquor and
starts walking towards the door.

PARKING LOT

Debra and Cynthia gets in their vehicles that are parked
beside each other. Cynthia drives off and Debra starts off
following her. Debra's vision starts to get blurry and then
loses sight of Cynthia. Debra swerves her vehicle off the
road. Debra turns her vehicle into a grassy field of green,
turns off her vehicle and falls asleep.

While Debra is asleep in her vehicle, she dreams.

INTERCUT DREAM SEQUENCE

                    DEBRA'S DREAM
          Debra is wearing glasses and the
          frame part of the glasses are
          broken, but not broken to where she
          cannot see out of them. Debra
          removed the glasses and put them
          back on forgetting the frame was
          broken. In Debra's dream she
          repeats the cycle of taking her
          glasses off after realizing they
          are broken three items.

Debra wakes up in a panic and looks at the clock. The clock
read 3:33am. Debra looks around and starts crying.

Debra gets out of her vehicle, walks around looking at her
vehicle and is relieved there are no damages.

Debra walks away from her vehicle and starts to talk to God.

                    DEBRA
          Lord, why do you keep saving me,
          when I am not worthy of you or your
          love. Right now I need you. I am
          lost Lord in this field of nothing,
          and such as my life which is
          nothing. Right now I give myself to
          you. I ask for your forgiveness of
          all of my wrong doing to myself and
                    (MORE)

                    DEBRA (cont'd)
          others. I no longer want to be of
          this world, but I want to live for
          you Lord. Lord, you are my today,
          tomorrow and forever. Lord, I vow
          to you to never call another person
          my forever. Lord, I am not fearful
          for I know you are here with me
          now. I will not be dismayed for you
          are my God. I know you will
          strengthen me and will hold me up
          with your righteous hand. Amen.

Debra gets into her vehicle and drives home in silence.

INT. BEDROOM - DAY

Debra walks upstairs to her apartment, walks inside and
closes the door. Debra closes her door, she sits on the
sofa, gets her phone out of her pocket and calls Christiana.

                    DEBRA
          Friend, I am so sorry. I messed up
          again. I got lost and did not know
          where I was.

                    CHRISTIANA
          What do you mean, you didn't know
          where you were.

                    DEBRA
          I was following this girl home last
          night and in the midst of following
          her, I got lost and ended up in a
          field of green.

                    CHRISTIANA
          My God. I am getting ready to head
          your way. Stay put.

                    DEBRA
          Okay.

Debra takes a shower and lies down. She then hears a knock
at the door. She gets up, walks towards the door and answers
it. Debra embraces Christiana.

                    CHRISTIANA
          It is going to be okay. At least
          you don't smell like a brewery.

                    DEBRA
          Laughs out loud. I showered before
          you got here. Do you want some tea?

                    CHRISTIANA
          Sure.

59.

KITCHEN

Debra goes to the kitchen and pours herslef and Christiana some tea.

LIVING ROOM

Debra hands Christiana her tea and then sits on the sofa with Christiana.

                    CHRISTIANA
So, tell me what happened.

                    DEBRA
I was out drinking at the poetry club. I saw a girl and I was supposed to have been following her home and I ended up getting lost. It was scary. I want to have a relationship with God. I know of Him, but I want to know him. I desire to have a personal relationship with him.

                    CHRISTIANA
Thank you God!! I am so happy for you friend.

                    DEBRA
It took me to get lost with nothing around me. There has been so many times where I could have been seriously hurt, hurt someone or dead. He saved and protected me through all of my craziness. The unhealthy relationships. I don't regret any of the things I have gone trough because it got me to this place of wanting to have a personal relationship with God.

                    CHRISTIANA
I have been praying for this moment for a very long time.

                    DEBRA
Thank you for being so patient with me when I didn't deserve the patience. You stick with me through it all. I know I frustrate you.

                    CHRISTIANA
My question is, what do you plan on doing with your new life?

                    DEBRA
I plan on living to please God and not man, pray for my gifts to be
                    (MORE)

                    DEBRA (cont'd)
          brought to the forefront, to be
          able to hear God and listen to Him.

                    CHRISTIANA
          What about the drinking and
          smoking?

                    DEBRA
          I am a work in progress. I will be
          praying for deliverance from
          homosexuality, drinking and
          smoking.

Christiana stands up, walks to the kitchen to read the
writing on the refrigerator quietly.

Debra gets up, walks and stands next to Christiana as she is
reading what is on the refrigerator.

                    CHRISTIANA
          Is it okay that I spend the night?

                    DEBRA
          Of course, let me get the spare
          bedroom ready for you.

                    CHRISTIANA
          Let me go downstairs to get my
          things out of the car.

                    DEBRA
          Okay, do you need any help?

                    CHRISTIANA
          No, I don't have much.

Christiana walks outside and sees Sherry sitting outside
alone.

                    CHRISTIANA
          Hello, how are you doing?

                    CHRISTIANA
          Hey, 'm doing good.

Christiana walks downstairs to her vehicle, grabs her things
and walks back inside Debra's apartment. She notice Sherry
no longer sitting outside.

                    CHRISTIANA
          Hey, I am going to jump into the
          shower.

                    DEBRA
          Okay.

Debra kneels down to pray and then gets into her bed and
quickly fall asleep.

Christiana comes out of the bathroom and goes into Debra's room, covers her up and kneels down to pray while holding her hand. Christiana stand up and then walks to her bedroom. Christiana kneels down next to the bed to pray, get up, gets into bed and then shuts the lamp light off.

Christiana's alarm goes off ad she wakes up and looks at the clock that reads 5:25am. She calls into the prayer line and puts the phone on speaker. Debra wakes up and goes into the room where Christiana is in to listen.

> DEBRA
> What are you doing awake so early.

> CHRISTIANA
> I'm on the prayer line, do you want to listen?

> DEBRA
> Yes. I sure do

Debra lies in the bed and covers herself up while listening in on the prayer line.

Debra looks at the clock and it is 6:30am, she gets up and goes into the kitchen to get a cup of coffee. She walks back into the room, sits on the bed and continues to listen. She finish her cup of coffee and sets it down and looks at her watch and it is now 7:30am, Debra and Christiana gets up and goes into the kitchen. Debra cook her and Christian breakfast as they are still listening in on the prayer line. As they start to eat their breakfast the prayer line ends.

Debra makes a phone call

INTERCUT PHONE CONVERSATION

> DEBRA
> Hello, can I schedule a session today.

> THERAPIST
> Yes, I have an opening in an hour

> DEBRA
> Okay, I will see you in an hour. Christiana will you go with me. You can wait in the waiting room for me.

> CHRISTIANA
> Sure

Debra and Christiana are in the vehicle. Debra drives to her session.

INT. DEBRA'S VEHICLE - DAY

                    DEBRA
Chrisitana remember the dream I told you about regarding the glasses. Well I had the same dream last night. What does it mean.

                    CHRISTIANA

It means there is a transformation of your life within the frames of the eye glasses.

                    DEBRA
Thank you. I think it is amazing how God blessed you with the gift of dream interpretation. How did you know you were blessed withe this gift?

                    CHRISTIANA
A friend gave me a reocurring dream she was having for years. She told me to let her know when I interpret it. I told her I was not a dream interpreter. She said, that is not what God said. So, I wrote her dream down as she gave it to me, sat it on my dresser and then walked away from it. Later, God audibly gave me the interpretation of her dream. Then I started dreaming more often than before. I am truly thankful for my gift, but it can be exhausting because I am constantly waking up writing down my own dreams.

Debra and Christiana gets out of the vehicle and walks inside the building.

INT. THERAPIST'S OFFICE - DAY

                    THERAPIST
Debra, you ready?

                    DEBRA
Yes.

Debra walks into the therapist's therapy room and the therapist closes the door behind Debra. Debra sits on the sofa, then takes her shoes off and grabs a pillow to hold in front of her.

                    THERAPIST
How has everything been going?

DEBRA
I have been dissatisfied as to how my life is going and the current situation.

THERAPIST
Tell me more about that.

DEBRA
I was out drinking and ended up trying to follow a girl I met home. I thought I was no longer attracted to women, but anyway. I ended up getting lost in the midst of following her home. I ended up waking up the next morning in a field of green with nothing aroud me but God.

THERAPIST
You say you were drinking. What happened before you initially started drinking?

DEBRA
I ordered four drinks, sat down and listened to poetry at this Poetry bar. One of the poems made me tear up because the poem was a reflection of me. And then I left the bar with a girl. I was going to follow her home, but got lost.

THERAPIST
So, those thought of the poem was emotionally overwhelming which drove you to drink alcohol, which you tried to suppress by drinking more alcohol and then leaving with a girl you did not know because you did not want to feel.

DEBRA
Yes

THERAPIST,
Yes, because those thoughts are tied to those emotions and those emotions are tied to those thoughts and you want to escape them, and the normal way for you to escape is by suppressing them. You were still feeling those emotions so you approached this woman. What else numbs you from feeling?

DEBRA
Sex. Me and the woman was gonna go have sex at her place.

THERAPIST
The young lady agreed to have sex with you, you two leave the poetry bar, you get lost in the midst of following her. Let's go back, you got into your vehicle under the influence of alcohol. At thar point you cannot decipher right from wrong and nor do you care.

DEBRA
Yes, to everything you just said. I feel horrible. I am trying to get closer to God and I allowed the enemy to creep into my thoughts

THERAPIST
I have an assignment for you. I need for you to make a list of the benefits of alcohol and a list of how alcohol can harm you and the people around you. I want you to find a bible verse that talks about alcohol. Your hour is up. I will see you next week.

DEBRA
Okay. Thank you.

THERAPIST
Remember to be mindful of your thoughts because they contribute to your actions and just because you are thinking it does not mean you have to act upon it. Remember to challenge those thoughts that don't lead to your desired outcome.

Debra comes out of the therapist office. Christiana gets up and they walk to the car

CHRISTIANA
How did your session go?

DEBRA
It went well. I talked to her about my drinking, getting lost while trying to follow a girl home from the Poetry Bar. I also told her I want to be closer to God.

CHRISTIANA
I am proud or you. You are willing to take the necessary steps to b a better version of you. Don't forget to show yourself some grace, everything will fall into place when you put God first.

DEBRA
Thank you and yes, I truly believe
and receive that.

INT. DEBRA'S APARTMENT - DAY

Christiana and Debra walk into Debra's place. Christiana walks to the spare bedroom and picks up her bags. She walks back to the living room, sets her things down and gives Debra a hug

CHRISTIANA
I know you got this and don't
forget to get on the prayer line
every Wednesday and Friday at
5:30am.

DEBRA
I won't forget. Thanks for being a
great friend and patient with me
all these years while I was going
through my mess.

CHRISTIANA
Of course!!

Christiana walks out the door.

Debra sits on top of her counter with a bottle of water, and her wipe erase marker. Debra jumps off of the counter after.

she takes a drink out of her bottled water.

Debra Writes on the refrigerator: I love me. I am beautiful. #Focus #Dreams #Purpose. Evil company corrupts good habits. It is too soon to quit. #goals. #Commitment. What you put in your life is what you are going to get out of it- Cause/ Effect. I choose balance, harmony and peace. Servitude, Love, Humility.

Flashbacks of calendar dates Debra started the prayer line--March 2021-current)and of Debra listening in on the prayer line while drinking coffee, driving to work and eating breakfast. The actual pictures of the vision board on Debra's refrigerator and bathroom mirrorare displayed.

Debra's phone rings.

INTERCUT PHONE CONVERSATION

DEBRA
Hello?

CHRISTIANA
Hey, I want to invite you to a live
prayer in the park.

                    DEBRA
          Okay, send me the date, time,
          location and I will be there.

Christiana texts her the location, date and time. Debra looks at her phone and reads the text message from Christiana.

INT. BEDROOM - NIGHT

Walks into her bedroom and kneels down to pray.

                    DEBRA
          Thank you Jesus for your
          unconditional love, grace, mercy
          and favor.

Debra crawls into bed.

INT. APARTMENT - DAY

Debra wakes up, starts packing and goes to the kitchen and there is a knock on the door. Debra walks to the door and opens it.

                    SHERRY
          Hey Chantrelle, how are you doing?
          I wanted to know if you wanted to
          have a beer with me.

                    DEBRA
          No, thank you. I am no longer
          drinking. Would you like to have a
          cup of coffee with me?

                    SHERRY
          Nope, more beer for me.

Sherry walks away leaving Debra standing at the door. Debra closes the door and picks up her bags and cup of coffee. Debra leaves out of he apartment and sees Sherry drinking beer alone.

                    SHERRY
          Come on Debra, have one beer with
          me.

                    DEBRA
          No thank you.

Debra walks past Sherry. She puts her bags in her vehicle and then gets into her car. Debra sits there for a moment thanking God for strength and asks for protection and covering as she is driving to her destination.

While Debra is driving, she reflects on how her life used to be. There are flash backs of Debra drinking and driving, moving out of Maliah's home and getting lost in the field of green.

Debra arrives at the park, gets out of the vehicle and looks for Christiana. She sees a group of peopel sitting on a pillow aroind a tree. Debra sees an empty pillow next to Christiana. Debra smiles big and goes to sit on the empty pillow.

Everyones covers their head while the host is praying out loud. The host allows everyone to speak and or give their testimony afterwards.

Debra stands up and asks if she can speak. The host asks Debra to stand.

>   DEBRA
>   (stands and says a
>   prayer, then reads her
>   poem)
>   I'd like to say this is a poem God
>   instructed me to write. To whom it
>   may concern, from one alcoholic to
>   a recovered alcoholic child of God.
>   My walk with sobriety had begun on
>   7/21/2021. Let me back up because I
>   can remember a day in May. God woke
>   me up at 4:30am, and told me I
>   needed to go to AA. I asked God
>   why, all I have to do is pray and
>   the thought of drinking would go
>   away. The longest I went without a
>   drink was three days. The drinking
>   and being alone started at five,
>   which consisted of me getting drunk
>   off beer and wine. According to
>   Ephesians 5:18 that reads, Do not
>   get drunk on wine, which leads to
>   debauchery". This verse describes
>   the lack of control of who I used
>   to be. A well groomed liar and a
>   junky. Let's move on to first
>   Timothy 4:1, "The spirit clearly
>   says some will abandon their faith
>   and follow deceiving spirits and
>   things taught by demons". Well that
>   was my experience. As you can see I
>   am here to spread God's word and
>   how he saved me through his grace,
>   favor and mercy. I always take my
>   God's advise, because obedience is
>   better than sacrifice. I went to AA
>   and listened to people talk about
>   their sobriety, how long they've
>   been sober, and then I stood and
>   said, "Hello my name is Maricia and
>   I am no longer an alcoholic". I
>   actually started feeling the
>   opposite of melancholic. Another
>   thing God told me to share, first
>   Peter 5:8, "Be self controlled and
>   (MORE)

DEBRA (cont'd)

alert. Your enemy the devil prowls around liking a roaring lion waiting for someone to devour". The power of God, my Father and you say your higher power. You act as if the big book is the bible. It is not God's book. The way you spit out what the big book say. Lay your big book down and pray, and get withe God's plan and pray the alcoholic away. "He knows the plans he has for you, plans to prosper and not to harm you, plans to give you hope and a future". Dang I'm on fire, that came from the book of Jeremiah, that's 29:11. I don't know about you, but I am trying to get to heaven. I can go on and on but I am going to end by saying, I apologize to all my family friends I hurt over and over. Man it is a blessing to be sober.

EXT. OUTSIDE

Debra fades away and the view is on the the people far away.

FADE OUT:

* SPOKEN WORD POEM WRITTEN BY, MARICIA DUHART

70.

www.ingramcontent.com/pod-product-compliance
Lightning Source LLC
LaVergne TN
LVHW082245060526
838201LV00052B/1821